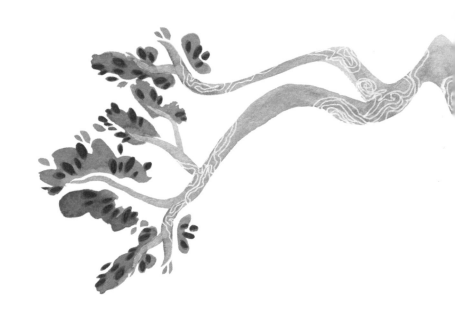

Seven
Sisters

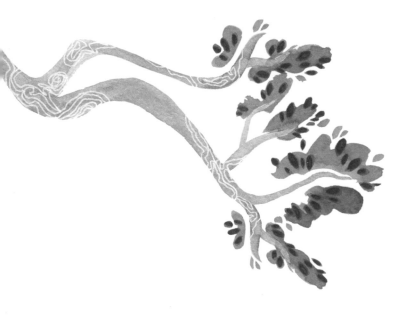

For the actual girls: Saffah, Esher, Amelia, Lola,
Zoha, Ayla and Zayna. May you all flourish,
wild and brilliant. ~ AM

For Laura, forever my sister. And for Tom, who believed
in me years before anyone else did, and helped me grow
until this book came along. ~ EM

Esher

Zoha

Ayla

Saffah

Zayna

Lola

Amelia

STRIPES PUBLISHING LIMITED
An imprint of the Little Tiger Group
1 Coda Studios, 189 Munster Road,
London SW6 6AW

Imported into the EEA by Penguin Random House Ireland,
Morrison Chambers, 32 Nassau Street, Dublin D02 YH68

First published in Great Britain in 2021

Text copyright © Ayisha Malik, 2021
Illustrations © Erika Meza, 2021

ISBN: 978-1-78895-209-5

The right of Ayisha Malik and Erika Meza to be identified as
the author and illustrator of this work respectively has been asserted
by them in accordance with the Copyright, Designs and Patents Act, 1988.

STP/2800/0402/0312
Printed and bound in China.

2 4 6 8 10 9 7 5 3 1

Seven
Sisters

Written by
Ayisha Malik

Illustrated by
Erika Meza

LiTTLE TiGER
LONDON

In the Forest of Tremendous Trees the sun rose in all its majesty. It shone on seven sisters who each lived in a tree of their own that they could call home. Out cartwheeled Amelia from her tree house, twirling and whirling as she shouted,

"Wake up, lazy ones!"

She always forgot that some of her sisters were not early risers.

Saffah waved a drumstick at Amelia. She banged on her drums, singing her morning song.

"The sun is shining.
Oh yeah, oh yeah!
So get up without whining.
Oh yeah, oh yeah!"

"Stop that noise," cried Lola, sticking her head out of the window. She rubbed her eyes. "I'll spray you." She got out her cans of paint. Her quick arm twirled as a rainbow of colours splashed, swished and swirled on the bark of her tree.

New graffiti for a new day.

Out came Esher rolling her eyes, but Ayla's headphones almost slipped off her head she was laughing so much at Saffah singing.

"All right, we get the picture," said Esher. "But Ayla and I need *quiet*." Esher was fixing her plans for a new rope bridge (even though the plan was already perfect).

"I guess so," whispered Ayla, but as usual nobody heard her. She was enjoying the music but she should get on with building her new weather drone that would look out for storms.

Then Zoha appeared, stretching and yawning, still half asleep, until she spotted some vines that were torn.

"I'll fix those," she murmured to herself, gathering twigs from the lower branches. A group of squirrels and rabbits scurried around her. They loved spending time with her, and Zoha loved having them to herself.

Zayna dangled her legs from the branch
of her tree, shaking her head as she
watched all her sisters and their usual
morning mayhem. She was a writer so
liked quiet, but sometimes needed this
noise to be inspired. Zayna placed
bright papers on her lap, took
up a pen and wrote a poem
that went with the beat
of Saffah's drum.

8

Amelia swung on her vine to check up on Lola. "Wow! I *love* your new artwork," she said.

Lola smiled and decided to forgive Amelia for waking her up so early.

Esher crossed over to Saffah's on
the rope bridge she'd made. She was
finishing building Saffah a new sound
system, which, Esher reminded Saffah,
had taken, "Twenty-two days, three
hours and fifty minutes to make."

"I need help," said Zayna to her shy sister, Ayla. "There's a tech whizz in my story. Does their character sound right?"

"That's fine," said Ayla, but as she read, she secretly thought *the tech whizz sounds awfully like me.*

Zoha tried not to laugh at Ayla's worried face. (Zoha hadn't yet read Zayna's story about the girl who kept her animal friends to herself…)

Every day the sisters visited each other tree to tree, using the rope bridges, swings and trampolines. But because they were so different, (some are born loud and some are born shy), they were happy to return home and practise their talents alone.

Then one puzzling day the ground
stirred and it shook. Birds flew from
their nests, insects scuttled about.

Something was changing
but no one knew what.

Out came the sisters, one by one from their trees.

"What's that?"
sang out Saffah.

"Something's
happening!"
cried Lola.

"No kidding,"
said Esher.

"Is that…?"
started Zayna, already
making notes.

Zoha gathered all the
animals around her.

The ground rumbled, the sisters tumbled,
then to their surprise up shot a tree.

It got bigger
and bigger.

It didn't stop growing until
the sisters were craning their
necks to see to the top.

It was the most beautiful tree in the forest. Better than *all* their trees put together.

After spending all day staring at, and talking about, the marvellous tree they went to bed, but none of them could sleep.

Each sister imagined the type of house they could build in the tree. How wonderful it would be to practise their talents in that kind of space! They could be the best…

"Grower of gardens!"

"Engineer!"

"Writer!"

"Gymnast!"

"Singer and musician!"

"Painter!"

"Technician!"

17

The next day, as the sun rose again, all of the sisters
(even Lola and Zoha who weren't morning people)
had the same idea and jumped out of bed.

Zayna snatched up her
notebook and ran,
her pockets stuffed with
pencils and pens.

Amelia danced and
flipped all the way there.

Esher used her motorized
cable car and sped up ahead.

Lola wouldn't be left behind, though she was weighed down with her paints.

Nor would Saffah with her bundle of instruments.

Zoha flew, carried by
her favourite birds.

Even Ayla hopped from branch to branch,
clutching her half-built drone.

21

They all ended up in the gorgeous new tree
with its metres of space and what
seemed like *miles* of greenery.

"It's like it was made for me," said Zoha to her animals, touching the primroses and daisies and vines snaking up the tree. "Look at all these gorgeous flowers."

Lola gasped. "It's so beautiful." She stared around her, thinking of all the art she could make.

Inspiration immediately struck Zayna. Of course, this is where she'd be the best writer.

"I could *really* use the room," said Amelia, somersaulting in the air and catching a vine that dangled above.

Saffah got out her electric guitar and began tuning the strings.

Esher knocked on the bark. "I could invent so much more here. After all, what I do is *important*. You all wouldn't even have been able to get to the tree without my inventions."

Ayla gulped as she mumbled, "Mine's the smallest tree ... and with all this space I could finish building my new dro—"

But before she
could finish Saffah
burst into song,
strumming her
guitar as she sang,

*"The sound here
is so great!
Oh yeah, oh yeah!"*

Lola started painting, much
to the sisters' distress.

Zayna wasn't happy so she spread out her papers and wrote a story about six silly sisters.

"Go and make that noise in your own home," called Zayna to Saffah. *"I'm trying to write."*

But Saffah only played louder.

Soon all the sisters were arguing with one another.

"Don't
dangle
over
me!"

shouted Zoha to Amelia.

28

The vine snapped and Amelia fell into
Lola's crate of paint.

"Oops!"

"My colours," Lola cried.

The paints exploded all over the place,
covering Saffah's guitar, Zayna's papers
and Ayla's drone and face.

There were too many of them,
it wouldn't do!

The sisters carried on arguing over one another.

They crashed

and they cried,

music blared,

colours burst.

Papers (and
tempers) flew.

Animals scampered around nervously but each sister stood their ground.

CRASH! BANG!

"MOVE IT."

"SHHHH, QUIET."

"I NEED IT!"

"ENOUGH, EVERYONE!"
Saffah called.

The sisters froze.

Saffah stood in the middle of her sisters, hair all over the place.

"You need a brush," mumbled Ayla, scraping paint from her face.

"Look who's talking," Amelia snapped.

Zayna piped up. "*Let's get a grip.* We obviously all *want* the tree, but we can't all *use* it."

After some more commotion an idea came to Esher. "Let's have a competition!" she said. (She was sure she would win.)

Each sister would show, by using her talent, who needed the tree more.

"And who will be the judge?" asked Zoha.

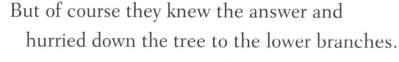

But of course they knew the answer and hurried down the tree to the lower branches.

They swung through the forest, rushing, pushing and shoving. They carried on arguing over the tree until they reached a big house where their dear aunt lived. They knew she would judge fairly.

(Each sister thought the aunt loved them the most.)

"Gosh, what a sight," said the aunt when she answered the door. The sisters looked like they'd fought with tigers and bears on their way.

But without a hello, they all barged in…

And at once they started shouting.

"This tree grew—" spoke Zoha.
"It's *gorgeous*," interrupted Lola.
"I want it!" cried Amelia.

"*Girls!*" exclaimed their aunt. "I know, I've seen it." She pointed
out of her window and they could see the sprawling branches
of the magnificent tree. "I don't understand," said the aunt.
"It's big enough for *all* of you."

"But we're so *different*," answered Zayna.

"Exactly! People who are different
can't all live togetherrrr," sang out Saffah.

"We did try," added Ayla.
"But … well … *look at us*."

The aunt stared at the
wild looking girls. She
couldn't believe it.
What had happened to
her lovely, talented nieces,
who always got along?

"We'll have a competition about who deserves
the tree and *you'll* be the judge," said Esher.

"*How?*" said their aunt.

"By, well, showing our talents," replied Ayla.
"We'll just need some time to prepare."

The aunt paused and gave it some thought.
"Are you *sure* this is what you want?"

"Please, please, *please*," they begged.

"All right!" said the aunt.
"But think of all the things
you could lose when
you're fighting to have
just one winner…"

The sisters went home under the glittering stars, while planning
in their heads how they'd win over their aunt. When they got
back to their trees it was time for bed, but instead of saying
"good night" to each other they all slammed their doors.

The next day
each sister woke up, ready
to prepare for the competition.
Their aunt was so worried she
surprised each niece with a visit. One by
one they tried to show-off the very, *very* best
they could be if only *they* got the new tree.

Lola painted her walls spectacular colours, with
drawings of all the beautiful things in the world.
Mountains and sunsets and (of course) forests.
"These paintings bring joy," she exclaimed.
"Shouldn't I get the new tree
so I can spread happiness?"

Amelia jumped and she
flipped before she landed
and did the splits. She
twirled so fast she became
a blur to her aunt.

"With my skills I grab the food we eat,"
said Amelia without stopping, "so the tree
should be mine or we'll all starve."

(Amelia had forgotten that Zoha also
grew food in her garden.)

Plants towered over her aunt as Zoha
explained, "The tallest tree should be
mine so I can keep watch because *I* look
after the forest. And," she whispered,
"I give so many animals a home."

On the floor kneeled Esher, measuring and planning. She had brought out every invention she had ever made (pretending her place always looked this way).

Her aunt tripped over wires as Esher said, "It's impossible to be *brilliant* when I'm always tumbling over things."

Saffah's music blared from her sound system (that she'd forgotten Esher had built). She blew on her trumpet and banged on her drums, got out her guitar and sang her aunt songs. "My music entertains us all and the sound in that tree is so good it's *insane*."

40

"Look at all these stories I've written," said Zayna. She made her aunt read *each* and *every* one. "People *love* hearing them. That's why they visit our forest. And *that's* why I deserve the tree."

Their aunt went to bed worried about how she'd decide. If only the sisters could see that although they were different, they were better together. And anyway, where is the joy in being the same?

On the day of the competition the sisters gathered in the forest. The sky was grey, a gale (like the sisters' moods) was brewing and getting wild, but they hardly noticed.

Until the wind grew so strong it nearly carried them away.

The trees in the forest swayed and they swung.

A strong gust blew Saffah's trumpet
and Lola's spray cans away.

Rain   showered

down.

A storm had begun!

No one's home looked safe but there
was one place they could go.

"To the big tree!"
Zoha cried.

The sisters scrambled after her,
pulling one another along as
they hurried to the tree.

44

The storm darkened the forest, the wind howled in anger.
It rained so hard no one could see from under the cover
of the tree's leaves and thick branches.

Trees cracked and fell,
animals hid wherever they could.

The rain came heaving and splashing, washing away all the things Zoha had planted. Esher's rope bridges twisted and turned until they finally broke.

Then a bolt of **thunder roared** and a blaze of **lightning shot** through the forest.

The girls huddled together, **supporting each other.**

(That's what sisters are for, whatever the weather.)

It felt like hours until one by one they all fell asleep, wrapped in each other's arms.

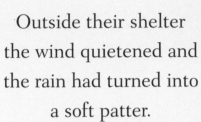

Outside their shelter
the wind quietened and
the rain had turned into
a soft patter.

Then morning broke
and the sisters woke.
A slice of light came
through the leaves.

They all rushed to the
ends of the branches.
Only to find…

Their forest in ruins.
Everything broken and washed away.

And the sisters' homes …

every single one …

gone.

Zoha sobbed,
Amelia blubbered.

For Saffah
all music had
stopped.

No story mattered to Zayna. All colours were grey to a tired and sad Lola.

"We'll fix this, you'll see," said Esher.

"Yes," answered Ayla, though she wasn't sure how.

The sisters were about to find out
that closeness could come out of chaos.

"I'll ge-get the a-animals to help," said Zoha between sobs.
"But *how will I find them?*"

The forest was so damaged the animals were all in hiding.

"I know!" exclaimed Saffah. She took out her tambourine
and shook it while singing a song.

The music travelled through the broken oaks and beaten
leaves, the birch and the elm, all of the fallen trees.

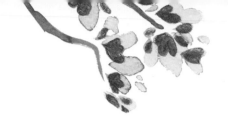

Out came the squirrels and foxes, the rabbits and ants.
The birds settled on Zoha's shoulders and around the girls
buzzed the bees.

Ayla thought for a while and finally said loudly, "Shouldn't we
be grateful that … that, you know … we were *together*.
Otherwise we really would have lost *everything*."

The sisters all paused and considered this for a moment,
patted Ayla on the back and replied, "Quite right."

Then Amelia shouted, "Let's get going!"

They still bickered (of course!), and each one thought *they*
were right (to be expected), but all had one goal…

To rebuild their homes.

Zoha tended to nature with even more care. And when tempers ran high or the girls disagreed, Saffah would play her music and sing them a song. Esher and Ayla designed the tree houses, while Amelia flipped and slipped through tricky places to get the materials for the sisters to put a new home together.

Each night they went to sleep in the big, new tree where they were building the *best ever* tree house. Now, somehow, there was room for everyone.

This didn't happen by accident.

Everyone agreed Zoha belonged at the top of the tree. Lola kept her paints in a crate. Amelia only used the vines on her side and Esher built Saffah shelves where she could keep her instruments.

56

Ayla finally finished her weather detection drone so there would be no fear of being surprised again by a storm.

As for Zayna, she realized she didn't need *that* much room, after all.

It took months and months, it sometimes felt like *years* (which is when there were tears), but the sisters worked together and never gave up.

They rebuilt their old tree houses as well as the new one. Soon the forest began to look like it used to. The sisters realized it wasn't a place or its space but its *people* that made a home.

Lola and Zayna had stuck together and helped wherever they could, but when their sisters' work was done, theirs had just begun. They wrote and painted on the walls of their new, big tree house, to show the ups and the downs, the good and the bad. Because time will pass, people and things come and go, but stories always live on.

The sisters found that they actually *liked* living together. Esher learned that nothing could be perfect and Amelia thought things through a little more. While Ayla learned to be louder and Saffah thought to be quieter.

Zayna began to write stories that *didn't* involve her sisters and Lola agreed to paint a portrait of the whole family. And even though it was hard, Zoha tried to share her animal friends.

This meant there was room for more people to come and share the forest, to live in the new tree houses that used to belong to the sisters. The forest soon became a home to lots of different people.

As for the sisters, they lived in a home
where they *liked* being different (the talent they
each *had* was not always what they *needed*).

A home where the girls' hearts
were even bigger than the
tree house they now
shared together.

About the author

Ayisha Malik's adult novels include *Sofia Khan is Not Obliged*, *The Other Half of Happiness*, and *This Green and Pleasant Land*. Ayisha was a WHSmith Fresh Talent Pick and *Sofia Khan* has been a CityReads London book. Her children's books include a re-telling of Jane Austen's *Mansfield Park* and *Seven Sisters*. She is the winner of *The Diversity Book Awards* and has been shortlisted for *The Asian Women of Achievement Award*, *Marie Claire's Future Shapers' Awards* and the *h100 Awards*.

Twitter: @Ayisha_Malik
Instagram: @ayisha82

About the illustrator

Erika Meza is an author and illustrator from Mexico. After studying graphic design back home, she moved to Paris to attend the Illustration (Image Imprimée) programme at ENSAD. She now lives with a French cat in the UK and works with ink, gouaches, watercolor pencils and Photoshop, fuelled by chocolate and incessant cups of coffee.

Twitter: @ErikaDraws
Instagram: @erikadraws